The adventures of
Artie the Airplane
and his friends™

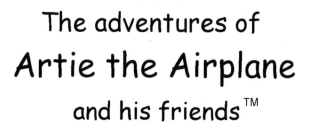

It's More Than
Just A Scarf

Written and Illustrated by
Captain Chuck Harman

"Ahhh!" said Jack the Jumbo. "Fall is in the air!" Jack looked around and saw trees turning beautiful colors, airport workers bundling up against the wind and all of the passengers eager to fly to warmer places.

As Jack waited for his passengers to finish boarding, he went over his checklist for the flight. "Let's see," said Jack. "We're going to Hawaii, so I need enough fuel. Check. Flight plan; check. Weather; check. Swim fins, inner tube, swim suit; check." Jack smiled to himself.

As Jack taxied onto the runway, he waved good-bye to the Big Town airport. "Good-bye Big Town, aloha Hawaii!" said Jack as he began his takeoff roll.

After several hours of flying, Jack landed in Hawaii. The warm tropical breezes felt good and Jack couldn't wait to get to the beach.

As Jack relaxed on the water, he thought about his buddy, Frankie, back home. "I wish Frankie could carry enough gas to fly here with me. He sure loves to surf," he thought. "Too bad he has to stay back at Big Town all winter long."

When Jack returned to the airport, he again thought of his friend, Frankie, and the coming winter. "I know!" said Jack. "I'll bring Frankie something from Hawaii—something he can use when it gets cold! I've got a little time before I have to get ready for the trip back. I'll go look around."

Down at the airline store, Jack saw a really great scarf. "I'll bet Frankie would like that," he thought. "It'll keep him warm. I'll get it for him!"

When Jack got home, he rushed over to Frankie the Fighter's place. "Hi, Frankie," said Jack. "Look what I got for you!" Jack was excited about the scarf he had bought for Frankie.

Frankie looked at the scarf and said, "Oh, I didn't want a scarf, but thanks anyway, Jack. Oh yeah, and Jack? You look kind of silly with all that stuff on."

Jack's feelings were hurt, so he pretended to be angry with Frankie and taxied away mumbling, "'Thanks anyway' . . . Hmmmph. I hope you're still saying 'thanks anyway' when the wind starts blowing this winter, Frankie!"
"Gosh, what's he so mad about?" thought Frankie.

The next day, Frankie stopped by Jack's place. Jack was still acting grumpy and Frankie thought it would be best to leave. "I'll see you later, Jack," said Frankie.
"Hmmmph," said Jack.

Frankie stopped by Artie's hangar. "Artie?" asked Frankie. "Do you know why Jack is mad at me?"
Artie said, "I don't know, Frankie. I haven't heard anything. Let's talk to Grampa Cubbie. Grampa Cubbie knows everything!"

Artie and Frankie taxied around looking for Grampa Cubbie.
He wasn't at the cargo ramp. He wasn't at the fire station.
Artie called the control tower and asked if they could see
Grampa Cubbie. The controller told him, "That's affirmative,
Artie. He's at the north end of the airport."

Artie and Frankie found Grampa Cubbie telling funny stories to some friends on one of the taxiways. "Excuse me, Grampa Cubbie," said Artie. "Could we talk to you for a minute? We need some help."

Grampa Cubbie said, "Sure boys, just a minute." He finished telling the other airplanes the rest of the story, then said, "Now boys, how can I help?"

Frankie told Grampa Cubbie about the scarf that Jack brought him from Hawaii. He explained, "I told Jack that I didn't want it, but I did tell him thank you anyway. He just got all mad and said something about the wind and taxied away."

Grampa Cubbie told Frankie that Jack probably seemed mad
because his feelings had been hurt. "What do you mean,
Grampa Cubbie? Why would that hurt Jack's feelings?" asked
Frankie.

"Think about it, Frankie. It's more than just a scarf. Jack was somewhere and he wished you were there, too. He spent his time and money getting you a gift because you couldn't be there. Instead of being excited about it and thanking him for it, you told him you didn't want it."

Frankie said, "I didn't mean to hurt Jack's feelings! He's my friend."

Grampa Cubbie told Frankie, "It's not the gift that you thank someone for, it's the thought. That person thought enough of you to take the time and effort to get you something. That's what you really are thanking them for."

Frankie looked around the airport until he found Jack. "Jack?" he said, "Thank you for getting me the scarf. I know you put a lot of thought into picking out the color and everything and I'm sorry I hurt your feelings. If you're not too upset with me, I'd like to try on the scarf—if you still want me to have it."

Jack said, "Sure Frankie, here, try it on!" Frankie tried on the scarf. It fit perfectly. "Thanks Jack!" said Frankie. "It feels great! Let's go flying!"

Jack and Frankie took off and Frankie pulled out in front of Jack. The wind was flapping the scarf behind Frankie and it was hitting Jack on the nose as they flew.

"Frankie?" asked Jack.

"Yes?" replied Frankie.

"I know you like the scarf and everything, but you don't have to wear it every time we go flying if you don't want to."

Frankie rolled over and turned around to look at Jack and saw the scarf flapping his friend on the nose. Jack and Frankie started laughing. They laughed so much they had to land.

Frankie wore the scarf all winter long. Every time he put it on, he felt a little warmer and he would always say to himself, "Thanks, Jack!"

Meet A Few Of

Alice the Air Ambulance

Albert T. Agplane

Becky the Big Tire Blimp

Bubba the Bush Plane

Carlos the Cargo Plane

Codi the Copter

Eduardo the Explorer

Frankie the Fighter

Gilda the Glider

Gramma Cubbie

Grampa Cubbie

Heidi the High Wing

Jack the Jumbo

Jessie the Jet Fuel Truck

Leslie the Low Wing

Artie's Friends

Pete the Patrol Car

Pierre the Plane

Piper

Robert the Rescue Plane

Lt. Sam Sweptwing

San Antonio Sal

Simon the Starfighter

Shirley the Skyvan

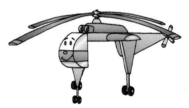

Sigmund the Skycrane

Superslim

Tina the Tailwheel

Waldo W. Wing

Wally the Widebody

Bartholomew T. Barnstormer

Captain Chuck

Artiefacts

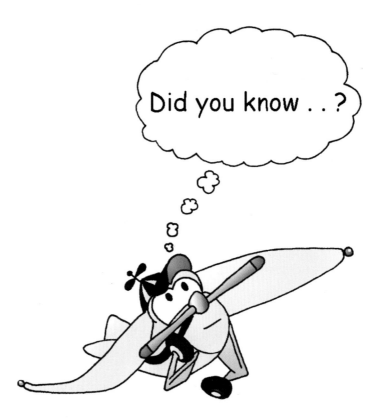

Modern jet airplanes can fly as high as 55,000 feet in the air. That's over 10 miles! At altitudes above 20,000 feet, the air is so cold that you can see the water vapor in the jet's exhaust. Because the water vapor condenses and becomes visible, it is called a "contrail" or "condensation trail."